RESISTING HER SHIFTER

A PARANORMAL COUNCIL STORY

LAURA GREENWOOD

To keep up to date with new releases, sales, and other updates, you can join my mailing list via my website or The Paranormal Council Reader Group on Facebook.

BLURB

She has everything she ever wanted, and now her fated mate is in her way.

Aella Dentro has always wanted to take her place on the High Council, but now she has discovered a problem...her fated mate.

Barker has been waiting his entire life for his mate to show up, but now she has, he's realised they can't seal their mating bond, not while both of them are working for the High Council.

Can they resist the connection between them? Or do they give in and risk losing everything they've worked for?

-

Resisting Her Shifter is a forbidden romance fated mates m/f paranormal romance featuring a snow leopard shifter and a nymph.

If you love fated mates, unusual shifters, witches, dryads, and a hint of steam, start The Paranormal Council series now!

PROLOGUE

Aella
A year ago...

AELLA ALMOST COULDN'T BELIEVE that she was finally here. It had taken years of working on the Nymph Council for her to finally have a chance to join the High Council who presided over all the paranormals in the UK. She was lucky a seat had even come open so soon. Many Council members held onto their seats for decades.

She walked into the Council building and past the Nymph Council door. It was a strange feeling not to turn into the room and go meet the other Council members, but she knew that wasn't an option. She couldn't serve on both the Nymph and High Councils. And rightly so. How could she pass down the laws that ruled over all paranormals when she was unduly biassed?

She reached the door marked for the High Council and took a deep breath. This was it. Her whole life was going to change when she stepped through it and into the room. Despite being ready for the change, she was nervous about it. What if the other Council members didn't like her?

She pushed that thought aside. There was no reason to borrow trouble from the future. She considered knocking, but decided it was better if she started as she meant to go on.

The door opened easily and led her into the Council chambers. Five large chairs filled the room, but only one of them was taken.

Aella repressed the disappointment welling up inside her that there weren't more members of the Council there to meet her. She'd have thought a new member would have needed something more than that.

The man in the lone filled seat got to his feet and stepped forward, a genuine smile on his face. "Welcome," he said. "I'm Barker."

"Aella."

"I know." He held out his hand for her to shake.

The moment their skin touched, a storm began to roll inside her unlike it had ever done before. She lifted her gaze and met the man's, surprised by the intensity lingering in them. It seemed that she wasn't the only one feeling strange about their meeting.

She cleared her throat and pulled her hand away. "Where's everyone else?"

"They thought it would be better if there was just one of us here to make it so that you weren't overwhelmed. There's a lot to do for your first day."

She raised an eyebrow. "I'm not some wilting flower new to politics," she pointed out.

Barker chuckled. "No, you're not," he agreed. "Your reputation precedes you."

"You make that sound like a bad thing."

"I assure you it's not. I've never heard anything bad."

"Now I know you're lying." But a small part of her enjoyed the flattery.

A small smirk played on his lips. "You've got me there. I'm sure you're aware that we do stringent background checks on all of the applicants for Council positions."

"I am, I already went through the process several times on the Nymph Council," she said.

Barker directed her towards one of the chairs, which she assumed was supposed to be hers.

She made her way over and stood in front of it, not quite ready to sit down, but knowing that she should. Something about this moment felt more underwhelming than she'd imagined it would.

"So, what can I expect from being on the Council?" she asked Barker.

"A lot of work." He grinned. "But it's worth it."

"That's what I'd hoped," she admitted. "This is something I've wanted for my entire life."

He chuckled. "I'm afraid you're probably going to end up disappointed. It's not nearly as glamorous as you might think."

"I'm not here for the glamour," she promised. "I'm here because I want to be part of changing the landscape for paranormals everywhere."

"Then you'd better get used to sorting out minor squabbles and screening Council applications. With everything going on with the Necromancer Council, we've had our work cut out for us."

"I can understand that." Knowledge of what had gone on with the Necromancer Council had spread like wildfire through the paranormal community. She'd have had to be living under a rock to miss it, and that was one thing no one could accuse her of.

"I heard that you were the youngest person to ever sit on the Nymph Council," Barker said.

"I was, but it's not as impressive as you might think. I only got the position because my father resigned his post."

"That isn't a guarantee of anything," he pointed out. "There would still have been the screening process to go through, and if they hadn't thought you were capable of the job, then you wouldn't have received it."

"True."

"That didn't take much convincing."

Aella's lips twisted into a smile. "I never said I didn't believe that I deserved the seat on the Nymph Council, just that I got it because of who my father was. If I hadn't deserved it, then I wouldn't have been in a position to apply for the High Council."

"A fair point. Confidence in yourself will go a long way when it comes to the other Council members."

"What are they like?" she asked.

Something about Barker put her at ease in a way no one else had. It vaguely reminded her of the way her sister talked about her mate, but Aella refused to believe that was possible. Two mates couldn't sit on the same Council, and she wasn't about to give up her seat now she'd gotten it.

"It depends on the day. Richard and Shelly are reasonably dependable, but Drummond can be a problem. He's still set in the old ways of doing things and doesn't like being convinced that anything modern could be the best option."

"It sounds like he should retire," she muttered, regretting it instantly. She barely knew Barker, his loyalties were a mystery to her.

Barker chuckled. "That's some people's opinion. He won't do it, though."

"Then it's a shame for paranormals everywhere."

"Mmhmm."

"So, what can I expect for my first day?"

"Just your contract and other paperwork to make sure you get paid correctly. I have it here." He leaned down and pulled out an alarmingly big stack of paperwork on the table between them.

She sighed loudly. "I guess I'd better get started."

"Can I get you a tea or coffee?" he offered. "At least that should make it go a little better."

"Tea, please. Two sugars and a dash of milk."

"Coming right up." The way he smiled at her made her heart skip a beat.

She shoved the feeling down. There was no doubt the man in front of her was attractive. He was just her type as well. Tall, with dark brown hair and a light smattering of stubble. But she couldn't go there with him, even if he was her mate.

Especially then.

She'd managed her life's dream, she wasn't going to let anyone ruin that.

ONE

BARKER

BARKER LEANED BACK in his seat as he listened to Richard talk about the progress the Paranormal Criminal Investigations department was making. As far as Barker could tell, nothing much had changed other than them opening another branch in Leeds. While he was interested in the possibilities surrounding crime-fighting in the paranormal sector, it was more as an abstract concept than the day-to-day running of it. He'd been glad that Richard had been the one to offer to take charge of it.

His gaze strayed to Aella, and she quickly glanced away.

Barker repressed a sigh. He'd always wondered about who his fated mate would be, but he'd never imagined that they wouldn't be able to act on it once they discovered their bond. But the Council rules were strict, and if they sealed their mating bond, one of them would have to give up their seat. She was too good at her job to lose hers, and he wasn't ready to give up his either.

But it still hurt to be in the same room as her and not be able to touch her. He wanted to be with her more than he'd ever wanted anyone before.

"Thank you, Richard," Shelly said. "It's good to hear that the PCI is doing well."

Barker repressed a smile. She seemed almost bored. He understood in a way, the PCI had taken up a lot of their Council conversations over the past few years.

"Now, moving on. The race track on the other side of town is getting ready for the grand opening. Aella, are you all right to check it out?"

"Of course," the dark-haired nymph said.

"I don't think Aella should be going alone," Drummond said, his customary scowl on his face. "The track is an important opening for us."

"I'm sure Aella is more than capable," Richard said. "She's been on the Council for a year already, and she's been here for all of the talks about the paranormal sports initiative."

"Hmm." Drummond leaned back in his seat, clearly unconvinced.

"I can go with her," Barker said before he'd had a chance to think it through.

Aella looked up sharply.

"I've wanted to see the track for a while now. Aella can deal with all of the Council matters while I look around, and if there's anything she needs assistance on, I'm there, which should satisfy everybody." He shot a look at Drummond, making it clear that he didn't want to hear any more protests from the elderly dragon.

"Fine," Drummond muttered.

Aella shot Barker a disapproving look, but he could only respond with an apologetic smile. He hadn't meant to make it so that they had to spend time together, but he wasn't about to backtrack on it now. He'd have to convince her that it was a good idea for them to work together sometimes or someone might start asking why they were avoiding one another.

"All right, I'll make sure that the information is sent over to both of you to look over," Shelly said.

"If Barker has better things to do, I'm happy to

do it on my own," Aella said. "I'm sure he's very busy."

"No, no," Drummond dismissed. "You need the supervision."

Aella scowled at the old dragon, clearly unhappy with his meddling. Barker didn't blame her. He didn't remember Drummond responding the same way when Shelly joined the High Council. Perhaps there was more to it that Barker wasn't aware of, but he doubted he'd ever find out. Drummond was more secretive than anyone Barker had ever met in his life. Even the dragon shifter who had been on the Shifter Council while Barker had served there had been less secretive than Drummond was.

"Very well. If you'd all excuse me, I have work to do." Aella got to her feet and left the room without saying another word to any of them.

The urge to growl rose within him but he pushed it down. His leopard side would have to behave, this wasn't the right time to claim his mate. It didn't matter how much they wanted one another, they couldn't do anything about it until they were ready.

Which meant that the best thing he could do to help Aella was to stay in his seat and not chase after her.

"That was unnecessary," Barker said to the

dragon. "Aella has been a part of this Council for a year and has done great work. You should let her do assignments on her own."

Drummond raised an eyebrow. "Perhaps if she does well at this one, I will reconsider."

Richard cleared his throat. "I think we can consider this her final task with supervision."

"I think that's a good idea," Shelly agreed.

"Me too," Barker said needlessly. He was reasonably sure that his views on the matter had been made clear to everyone present.

They all turned their attention to the dragon, waiting for him to voice his opinion.

Drummond sighed loudly. "I see I have been outvoted."

Richard smiled, the victory plain on the vampire's face. "Excellent, so this will be Aella's final supervised assignment."

Barker sighed with relief. He knew Aella was capable of fighting her own battles, but sometimes it didn't hurt to put in a good word.

"Barker," Richard said.

"Hmm?"

"Why don't you go tell Aella the good news?" There was something in the way that the other man smiled that made Barker think that he knew something was going on between him and the storm nymph. "I think we're done here." He looked between the other Council members as if challenging them to say to the contrary.

"I can," Barker said, trying to keep his excitement under wraps. He didn't want any of the others thinking that anything was amiss.

"Excellent. I look forward to reading Aella's report on the race track."

Barker took it as the dismissal that it was. Despite Drummond's belief that he was in charge, Richard was clearly the one with the actual power. Not that any one of them was supposed to be the leader. Each seat on the High Council was supposed to hold the same amount of political weight. Not that it ever worked like that.

Or that Barker thought the current power structure would stay in place for long. He had no doubt that Aella would be in charge of everything before long. She was the kind of person that people automatically listened to.

He said his goodbyes to the other Council members and left the room, heading towards Aella's office with a mixture of excitement and trepidation. As much as he wanted to see her, he also knew that being alone in an enclosed space would tempt them both. It was almost unbearable to be in the same room as her, but it was also painful to be away from her.

One day, they were going to push themselves too far and they would snap. But for now, they would carry on the way they were and hope for the best.

TWO

AELLA

AELLA SIGHED and put her papers to the side. As much as she'd always wanted to be part of the High Council, she'd never realised just how much work it was. While she was on the Nymph Council, she'd been able to keep her full-time employment too, but that was impossible when it came to the High Council. At least they got paid for this one. It would be impossible to do their job without it.

A knock sounded on her door, pulling her attention from her work.

Barker leaned against the doorframe with a boyish grin on his face. "Do you have a minute?"

She paused, not knowing whether she wanted to say yes or no. On the one hand, she always wanted to spend time with Barker. On the other, she knew it was dangerous to do so unless they wanted to end up mated. And from the way things stood, it seemed like neither of them were ready for that.

But seeing him standing in the middle of her office always made her question that.

"Come in," she said.

He stepped inside, closing the door behind him. Her mouth went dry at the thought of what they could do while they were alone.

She pushed the thoughts aside, knowing they were only going to make things harder.

"I'm sorry about the meeting."

"Don't be, I know what Drummond's like by now." She offered him a tight smile.

"Actually, that's what I came to talk about." He moved closer to her desk but didn't sit down.

"Richard put it to a vote about whether or not this should be your last supervised job for the High Council. After we're finished with the race track, you'll be free to do things on your own."

A small part of her wanted to rebel against the fact that the others had chosen her fate for her, but the more rational part knew that sometimes it was worth letting other people stand up for her.

"Thank you, I appreciate that."

"But there's nothing I can do about coming to the race track with you."

She sighed. "I think that's okay. It's not really my thing anyway, at least you'll enjoy it. All I'll be thinking about is the permits." They were starting to get on her nerves more than she wanted to admit.

"I've heard there are a couple of good drivers interested in the opening event, that should make it interesting."

"I'm glad about that, but I don't see why we need a race track in the first place."

"Because we can't race against humans."

"Yes, when it comes to physical sports. When everyone's in cars, I don't see what difference it actually makes," she muttered.

Barker shrugged and made his way over to her, perching on her desk. "Our reflexes tend to be sharper," he pointed out. "That means we can react to things that humans can't."

She sighed. "True."

"And we can heal faster."

"I'm not sure how that helps."

"It means paranormal drivers can take more risks. They don't have to worry about the consequences quite as much."

"Hmm. I don't think that's a good enough reason to be reckless."

"Perhaps not. I've never had the urge to race myself, but I understand the appeal of doing something for the adrenaline surge."

"Like agreeing we spend time together in front of the rest of the Council?" She got to her feet, which only brought them closer together. If she leaned forward, she'd be able to kiss him. Something she both did and didn't want.

"They'd get suspicious if we never did anything together too," he pointed out.

"No, they wouldn't. You almost never work one on one with Richard, no one thinks anything of it"."

"I don't think my expertise lends itself well to law enforcement."

"Nor to filling out forms apparently," she muttered, picking up a set he'd submitted the week before. "These are all wrong." She pushed them towards him.

A cheeky grin spread over his face. "Or are they wrong because I knew it would give me a reason to come and talk to you?"

Despite herself, Aella let out a small chuckle. "You're going to get us caught." Not that they were doing anything wrong so long as they didn't touch. But it was a technicality she wasn't ready to risk.

"And would that really be so bad?" He reached out and circled her waist with his arm, pulling her against him so their bodies were flush.

Her breathing hitched and a pleasant stormy sensation started to grow within her. He was impossible to ignore, even when she wanted to.

She cleared her throat, determined to remember what was at stake here, even if she wanted to give in. "Considering we'd both lose our jobs, yes."

"It's a silly rule."

"I don't disagree." She'd never really thought about the law against mates sitting on the same Council until it had started to affect her. But now she had, she realised how strange of a rule it was, especially when it excluded people who might otherwise be perfect for the job.

"It's not our fault we're fated mates," Barker said softly, reaching out and brushing a strand of hair behind her ear.

She didn't need him to remind her that even if they chose not to act on their mating bond, it didn't change the fact that it existed. One wrong move and they would still lose their jobs, even if they didn't do anything on purpose.

Aella glanced at the door and took a shaky breath. "One kiss."

Shock registered on his face. She'd never

suggested it before, and had always sworn she wouldn't, but the desire was too strong to ignore and she didn't want to wait a moment longer.

"Are you sure?" he asked, nerves coming through his voice. Or was it need?

She bit her lip and nodded. "I know we shouldn't." But that wasn't going to stop her. They'd come close to kissing a few times, mostly when the connection between them became too much to ignore.

And right now, the need to kiss him was even stronger than it had been those times, especially with how close they were. She supposed they could stand further apart in an attempt to stop themselves, but it was exhausting not giving in to him like she wanted to.

"Please kiss me." She knew he'd need to hear the words out loud before he did anything.

This wasn't how she'd imagined things to be with her fated mate, but she appreciated how conscious he was of her wants and needs.

Her eyes fluttered closed as Barker leaned in and brushed his lips gently against hers. The soft touch was already almost too much, but she could sense there was better to come and wasn't about to waste it.

She wrapped her arms around his neck and

deepened their kiss, nibbling on his bottom lip until he moaned softly into her mouth.

Desire rose inside her, demanding that they go further and properly seal the mating bond. But she resisted, unsure whether people would be able to tell what they'd done.

But it would be so good to let go.

"Aella…"

The way he whispered her name against her lips sent a shiver of need down her spine.

"I want you." The words slipped out without her thinking about them, but she couldn't bring herself to regret them.

Barker tugged her shirt from her waistband and slipped his hand underneath it, his fingers trailing over the smooth skin of her back.

It was a simple touch, but it made her want even more.

She was about to ask for it when her phone rang loudly, making both of them jump and pull back from one another. She stared at him with wide eyes that she imagined were still full of desire.

"Phone, Aella." His voice was hoarse and gruff, which only made her think of what it might sound like in the mornings when he'd just woken up.

Oh, how she longed to know what that was like.

She shook her head and turned to grab the

phone from the cradle. Barker stepped away, putting some much needed space between them.

Despite knowing it was better for them to not act on it, she couldn't help but feel disappointed.

It was only going to be a matter of time before they gave in completely.

THREE

Barker

RICHARD POPPED his head around Barker's office door. "Are you free?" he asked.

"I have a meeting at two, but I have time until then, I'm only filling out a report." He made sure to save his document before the other man entered the office. While he was reasonably sure it would auto-save, he didn't want to take any risks. Filling out reports could be tedious at the best of times, he didn't want to have to repeat the same ones he'd already filled out.

"Perfect, it won't take long." The vampire

stepped inside and made his way over to Barker's desk. He pulled out the chair and sat down.

"Is something wrong?" Barker asked, a little concerned about why the vampire was in his office, the two of them normally dealt with different parts of Council business and they didn't often overlap.

"Not really," Richard responded, leaning back in his seat and looking instantly at home in it. Barker had noticed that about the vampire before. He had this way of making it seem as if he was comfortable in just about any situation. "I wanted to talk to you about Narcissa and Darius."

Barker frowned. "The necromancers we tasked with regrowing the Necromancer Council?"

"Yes."

"Okay. I thought they'd done a good job?"

"They have," Richard assured him. "Which is interesting when they're technically breaking the rules by being on the same Council."

Barker froze, uncertain about what Richard was trying to get at and why this was relevant now.

"Anyway, it got me thinking about whether or not the rule is a good one," Richard continued as if Barker had responded. "If having it means that we lose a good person from one of the Councils, then is it a good thing?"

Barker cleared his throat. "I thought Darius had

made it clear that he intended to resign?" That was the way things stood the last time they'd discussed the issue.

"Hmm, he did. But it's not the first time we've lost a good Council member to something like this, there was something similar that happened to the Shifter Council just after you left, wasn't there?"

"Ah, yes, you mean with Arabella and Bjorn."

"Yes, that rings a bell," Richard said. "I heard that they managed to keep their mating bond quiet for a while but then it got too much and they gave in."

Something about the way the other man was looking at him made Barker think he was hinting about knowing more than he was saying with his words.

"I heard the same," Barker responded carefully. "And that it was Bjorn who ultimately resigned." He remembered the bear shifter from his time on the Shifter Council and hadn't been surprised to hear about his resignation. He'd never seemed particularly happy about sitting on it most of the time.

"Hmm. I can't help but think there must be a better way," Richard said. "I've tried bringing it up with Drummond before, but you know what he's like, he wants to know what laws and texts we have to back up a change. I've never had a chance to look in the Council library to find any, but I'm sure they're there."

Barker raised an eyebrow. "What makes you think that?"

A small smile pulled at the corner of Richard's lips. "Call it a hunch. Anyway, I'd better be going. I have a lot to do before my next meeting." He got to his feet and headed towards the door.

"Was that all?" Barker asked.

Richard turned to face him, a knowing expression on his face. "I think that's all you needed." Without another word, he left the room.

Barker leaned back in his chair, mulling over the vampire's words. There was a chance this was really about the necromancer mated couple, but he doubted it. Richard was a perceptive man, and mated himself, the chances were high that he'd noticed what was going on between Barker and Aella but didn't want to put him in an awkward position by outright saying it.

Without thinking twice about it, Barker picked up his office phone and dialled Aella's extension.

"Hello?" The sound of her voice made his heart skip a beat even down the phone.

"It's me."

"Barker..." She sighed loudly.

"I know what you're going to say."

She chuckled. "You can't possibly."

"You're going to tell me that it's too dangerous for the two of us to talk in private, even if it's over the phone."

She paused and he could imagine her biting her lip as she thought over what to say next. "No."

"Oh?"

"I was going to tell you that our kiss was a bad idea but I can't stop thinking about it."

"Me neither," he admitted. "But I might have a solution."

"To thinking about our kiss? I know it's a risk, but I'd rather keep my memories of it." The phone line crackled, but it wasn't enough to obscure her words.

"That's the last thing I want," he promised. "But I think we might be able to find some kind of past precedent that means we can both stay on the High Council and seal our mating bond," he said.

"Are you serious?" Her words came across as barely a whisper. "I didn't think that would be possible."

"I didn't either, but I think there might be something in the Council library."

"I can do a search on the database," Aella suggested.

He shook his head before realising that she couldn't see him. "I think we should search the records ourselves to make sure we're seeing the most accurate ones." He assumed there was a reason that everyone believed that mates couldn't sit on the same Council. Perhaps it was a record that had gotten lost or muddled up in the process.

"Okay. I'm free now if you want."

Disappointment flooded through him at knowing he could be spending time with her now but that he had another commitment. "I have a meeting, but I can meet you at four?"

"Okay. Four it is. I'll see you then." There was a slight pause. "I'm looking forward to it."

"Me too," he admitted.

"See you soon, Barker." She almost purred his name, making his inner leopard sit up and pay attention.

The phone beeped, signalling that she'd hung up before he'd had a chance to respond. Hopefully his meeting wouldn't overrun and he'd be able to get to the library on time to meet Aella. Once they were there, all they had to do was find something that said they could both keep their Council seats and then they'd be able to properly be together.

Right now, he wanted nothing more.

FOUR

AELLA

AELLA MADE her way through the Council building towards the archives, wondering whether she was making the right decision by meeting Barker there. She assumed he wouldn't have asked her to join him if he didn't have a good reason.

But that didn't make it any safer to be somewhere alone with him, not when almost every thought she had resulted in the two of them entwined together in a way she couldn't allow.

It was her own fault. If she hadn't asked him to kiss her, then this wouldn't be a problem in the first place. But now she had the memory of his lips against hers. She wanted more, but knew she couldn't have it. Not if she wanted to keep her seat on the High Council.

She checked over her shoulder to make sure no one saw her go inside, though she wasn't sure why. As a Council member, she wasn't going anywhere she wasn't allowed. The archives were a useful resource even if most of them had been digitised by now.

"You came." There was a note of surprise in Barker's voice, as if he didn't expect her to.

"You said it was important," she pointed out. "If it's not, I have plenty of work to do." She started to turn towards the door.

"It is," he assured her. "I think we might be able to find something in the archives that will allow us to act on our mating bond and keep our seats on the Council."

Her heart skipped a beat. If he was serious, this could change everything. "Do you really think we're going to find the answer to our mating problems in here?"

Aella stared at the towering shelves in front of them. Even from the entrance, she could tell that there weren't any people in the room, which was probably a good thing.

"I don't know," he responded. "But something

Richard said made me think this was where we'd find the answer."

Her blood ran cold. "You talked to Richard about us?"

"It was more that Richard talked to me about us. And not specifically. I don't know if he's figured out it's you who is my mate. He might just think it's one of the lower Council members."

"Which would also be a problem."

"Potentially a bigger one," he said.

She raised an eyebrow.

"If my mate was on a lower Council, then there'd be a potential for bias without meaning it."

"Hmm, good point." They made their way through the library. Despite the vastness of the information inside, there wasn't anyone else around.

"Have you been in here before?" Barker asked.

She shook her head. "There was never a reason to." She'd had access to all of the files on the database, there was never any reason to come in here. "But I've wanted to. There's something about libraries that I love."

"Maybe it's the amount of political information contained within."

She let out a soft snort. "More likely it's the fact that while I was at university all I wanted was to be one of those people making out in the shelves."

He flashed her a surprised look. "I'd have expected you to have thought of libraries as sacred."

She looked at him with a small smirk on her lips. "I never said I acted on it. Though a part of me still thinks about it every now and again."

"Interesting." His voice sounded just the way she wanted it to, interested but cautious.

"Do you think anyone will come in here?" she asked, glancing at the door.

Barker shook his head. "I don't see why they would. Why?"

"I was just thinking that perhaps you'd like to make one of my fantasies come true?" She raised an eyebrow.

"I thought you said it was too risky for us to kiss again?"

"I did, but I also haven't managed to think about anything since. Besides, being in the same room as you is risky." She stepped backwards between two shelves and crooked her finger. "Are you coming?"

He didn't hesitate and followed her into the more private area. She spotted a sturdy looking table and hopped up onto it.

"Are you sure about this?" Barker asked.

"Do you want to kiss me?" she responded.

"Yes."

"And I want to kiss you," she stated. "And we're all alone, no one is going to catch us."

He stepped closer to her and put his arms on either side, caging her in. "You're tempting fate there," he murmured.

"Maybe, but fate has been tempting me for long enough, now I'm just going to return the favour."

He was so close that his low chuckle almost felt as if it vibrated through her. She put her arms around his neck and waited for the moment when his lips would touch hers and she'd give in fully to the temptation he posed.

Her eyes fluttered shut and he stepped even closer, the heat of his body almost too much for her to ignore. How had she spent so long avoiding this? He was everything she'd ever dreamed of, even if he was standing in the way of her career.

Without meaning to, she trailed her hands down his chest and started to unbutton his shirt. Barker did nothing to stop her, even going as far as making it easier.

A small groan escaped her as she felt the hard planes of his chest and longed to explore more.

"Aella," he mumbled into their kiss. "You're going to have to stop if you don't want me to claim you right here and right now."

"Then I don't want to stop," she whispered.

Barker stepped back, breaking their contact and leaving her feeling suddenly cold.

"I'm sorry," she started.

He shook his head. "Don't be, I just wanted to give us a moment to make sure this is what we wanted."

She bit her lip. "Is it bad to say it is?"

"I don't think so," he responded. "Whether we act on the bond or not, we're already mates."

"That's true."

"It could be enough for the others to decide that we aren't allowed to both keep our seats. That's going to have happened at some point, whether we want to admit it or not," he said.

"And we're here to find a solution, right? It won't matter when we seal the bond if we find that."

He chuckled. "You're just finding a reason to sleep with me now, aren't you?"

Aella raised an eyebrow. "Am I that transparent?"

"Only in the best way." He stepped closer again. "But if you're sure about this, then I am too."

"I'm sure." She reached out for him and pulled him closer.

He leaned in and pressed a kiss against her lips. It was soft at first, full of emotion and anticipation, but it soon grew in intensity.

She pushed his shirt down his arms so it fell to the library floor. Knowing where they were only made the excitement build faster inside her. She didn't know whether it was because they were risking getting caught, or because of what it meant to her to be in the Council building, but this felt like the right place for them to be sealing their bond.

They made short work of their clothes, not caring where they fell.

Barker trailed kisses down her neck at the same time as smoothing a hand up the inside of her thigh. She parted her legs, allowing him closer. She was so ready for him that she didn't think she needed more teasing. Not that she was going to turn it down either.

His fingers teased her entrance and she let out a loud moan, tipping her head back. He moved them slowly and curled them upwards, hitting the precise spot she needed to send her crazy.

"More," she demanded.

He chuckled against her neck, but didn't deny her.

She did everything she could to keep her release at bay. If she wasn't careful, she was going to explode before they were properly joined together.

"I need all of you," she said. "Now."

He nodded and pulled his fingers from her. She glanced down in time to see him palm himself.

She bit her lip and watched with bated breath as he guided himself to her entrance. She'd never paid as much attention to this part, but there was something undeniably intense about it.

He entered her slowly, filling her in a way she'd never felt before. They fit perfectly together.

Her release was so close that she could almost taste it, only to be heightened by the sensation of the growing storm magic inside her. She'd been able to control it since she was a child, but right now she knew that she didn't stand a chance.

"Barker," she murmured. "More." She raked her nails down his back, being careful not to press too hard.

He shuddered against her, and she could tell he wasn't going to last very long. That was okay with her, she was close herself.

"I'm going to bite," he whispered, his lips grazing the soft skin of her neck, the sensations only adding to the building release inside her.

"Do it," she responded through shallow breaths. "Bite me."

He didn't need more than that. The sharp prick of fangs against her skin didn't hurt like she'd thought it might, but it did make it impossible for her to maintain any control.

The storm burst from her, crackling lightning engulfing their bodies. For a moment, she wondered if she'd done something wrong, but then realised this was just her magic's form of biting. She let it rage, and in the process sent herself over the edge.

Her whole body began to shake and she cried out, not caring in the slightest that they could end up caught. It was worth it.

Barker was worth it.

She clutched him tightly and pulled him over the edge with her. It didn't matter that it was all over quickly, it had been the most intense thing she'd ever experienced, and they'd have plenty of time to explore one another at leisure later.

And she planned to do precisely that.

FIVE

BARKER

To BARKER, the storm nymph looked more beautiful than ever. He didn't know whether it was her tousled hair, or the fact she'd left her suit jacket off and some of her buttons undone. She was always beautiful when she was smartly presented, but this was another look on her, and one that he hoped he'd get to see more of.

"You're watching me and not reading the books again," Aella pointed out without even looking up from the one she had in front of her.

"Sorry, my mind is starting to wander." He rubbed his temple. While that wasn't the only reason he was watching her, he had hoped it would help with the growing tension and frustration in his head.

"We could always take a break," she suggested with a raised eyebrow, her expression leaving no doubt about what she planned to do with that break.

"You're insatiable," Barker teased.

"What can I say? I was dying of thirst and now I want to quench myself."

"Please tell me you didn't just say that."

She grimaced. "It wasn't my best line, was it?"

"Luckily for you, I'm the only person who heard it."

"And you know better than to repeat it to anyone else." She fixed him with a stern look that only made him want her more.

"We should check a few more books and then call it a night," he said. "You have an early meeting with one of the drivers who is interested in opening the track, right?"

Aella sighed. "I do. And I'm looking forward to it. Sort of."

"Oh?"

"She sounds like an interesting woman. And you'll never guess what kind of shifter she is."

He had to admit that was an intriguing question.

"From the way you're saying it, I have to assume that a cheetah shifter is out?"

Aella chuckled. "Not even close."

"Oh, maybe something that normally lives in water?" That wouldn't be his first choice when it came to who he thought would gravitate to motor racing.

"Close, but not close enough."

"All right, you're going to have to tell me."

"She's a tortoise shifter."

Surprised flickered through him. "Really? I would never have gotten that."

"Me neither," Aella admitted. "But I kind of like the irony. They say she's been giving the male drivers a run for their money in the races, and everyone knows they need it."

"I thought you didn't understand the point of racing and why we needed a paranormal race track?"

"Let's just say that the more work I'm doing on it, the more I'm starting to appreciate the sport."

"Ah, so you might actually enjoy going down to the track on Thursday?"

"Potentially. But I'll enjoy it more if I get to go openly as your mate." She glanced away as if she'd said something wrong.

"I know the feeling," he admitted quietly. "I want nothing more."

Aella sighed. "Then why don't I go order some food and we can spend a couple more hours trawling through boring legal documents?"

He chuckled and ran a hand through his dark hair. "I thought you liked this kind of thing?"

"Normally, yes. When I'm having to stare at the tiny cramped handwriting and years of bad recording keeping, not quite so much." She rose to her feet. "Any preference for food?"

"Meat."

She smirked. "I could have guessed that. Am I going to start needing as much of it as you do?"

"I don't know," he admitted. "I'm surprised you haven't started craving more already."

"We only sealed our mating bond a couple of hours ago," she pointed out. "I doubt I'll be able to turn into a leopard tomorrow either. Though that would be pretty cool, I've always looked good in spots." She started to make her way past him.

He stopped her in her tracks and pulled her down so she was perched on his knee. "You'll look even better out of spots."

"Is that the shifter equivalent of *that dress will look better on my bedroom floor*?"

He grinned wickedly. "Do you want it to be?"

"I can't say I'm opposed to the idea." She leaned in and pressed her lips against his.

His desire for her grew, and he was certain she knew it from the way she squirmed against him. As hard as it was to pull himself away, he knew he had to if they wanted to get this done.

"Aella," he said softly.

She pulled back and let out a loud sigh. "I know. But once we're done here, I'm going to insist you take me back to yours."

He chuckled. "Your wish is my command."

"Excellent." She got up and straightened out her skirt. "I'm going to go order pizza. Will a meat feast do for you?"

"It sounds good."

"I'll be right back." She kissed his cheek before walking away.

He twisted in his chair to watch her go, admiring the way her hips swayed. She was probably doing it on purpose in an attempt to get his attention.

Aella glanced over her shoulder and smiled at him, confirming his suspicions. Not that he minded. He liked this more playful side of her, and was glad he had the rest of his life to explore it more and get to know her better.

With a loud sigh, he turned his attention back to

the book in front of him before slamming it shut
when it didn't reveal the information he needed.

He grabbed the next one from the stack and
flicked through it, scanning each of the sections in
turn in the hope that he'd find what he needed.
When that one proved useless, he closed it and
moved on to the next.

Aella returned to join him and picked up a
book of her own, and before long their pizza
arrived. His stomach growled, reminding him
that it had been too long since he'd eaten
anything. But he didn't want to stop his search
for the rules that would let them be together and
keep their seats on the Council. It was important
to both of them that they could, and he didn't
want to give up his position any more than
Aella did.

He was about to shut the book he was reading
when a small sentence caught his eye. Excitement
grew within him as he flicked over the page to see if
there was more information on the other side that
would help them.

"Aella?" His voice shook with cautious
excitement.

"Hmm?"

"I think I found it."

"What?" Her chair scraped back and she hurried

over to him, looking over his shoulder at the book in front of him.

The scent of a brewing storm filled the air, causing his inner leopard to sit up and take notice. He loved the way she smelled and hoped it wouldn't change too much when their magic mingled more.

"This bit?" she asked, pointing to the paragraph he'd just read.

He nodded.

"That says that if mates meet before they sit on the same Council, then they can't apply to belong to it." He could hear the confusion in her voice.

"Yes."

"But how does that help us?"

"Because it implies that if we meet because of the Council, then we don't have to give up either seat."

She chewed on her bottom lip. "Are you sure?"

"Honestly, no. But I think it's the best we've got. And Richard will support us wanting to change the rules."

"Drummond won't."

"Maybe not, but he'll be forced to agree if Shelly can be swayed to our side."

Aella sighed. "I have no idea if she'll be swayed."

"Shelly runs on logic and facts more than anything else. If we're able to prove that Arabella and Bjorn sat on the Shifter Council at the same time and made sound decisions, and bring up how well Narcissa and Darius worked together in re-establishing The Necromancer Council, then I think she'll be swayed to our side."

"Then let's push through and get everything we can together," Aella said. "I'd much rather spend the evening in bed with you, but what's one night compared to the rest of our lives?"

He smiled reassuringly at her. "Exactly. Why don't you go and find the records from Narcissa and Darius' time on the Necromancer Council and I'll go find the Shifter Council records for Arabella and Bjorn."

Aella nodded. "Divide and conquer."

"Exactly."

She leaned in and kissed him swiftly. "Then let's get this done so we can go home."

He was on his feet within moments, the promise of what was to come enough to propel him into action. Hopefully, they'd be able to find everything they needed, and then they'd be able to convince the rest of the High Council to let them keep their seats.

SIX

AELLA

AELLA'S HEART pounded as she waited for the other members of the High Council to read through the notes and evidence she and Barker had managed to compile. This was make or break for them. At the end of the meeting, they'd either both have their seats, neither of them would, or they'd be forced to choose which of them was going to give up theirs.

She didn't like either of the latter two options, but she knew it was impossible for them to continue as they were, especially after sealing the bond between them. All it would take was one slip up and their secret would be out in the open.

It was making her even more nervous to be standing in the middle of the room and not sitting in her chair. At least she had her mate by her side and didn't have to worry about going through this alone.

As if he sensed her thoughts, Barker reached out and took her hand in his, giving it a gentle squeeze. Her first instinct was to pull hers away and break any contact between them so it wouldn't be obvious that they were together, but then she realised the whole point of them being here was so that they could be a couple out in the open as well as behind closed doors.

"It'll be okay," Barker promised her quietly.

She nodded, though she wasn't quite sure she believed him. Not because she thought he'd lie to her, she knew he wouldn't do that. But more because it was impossible for them to be certain of anything.

Richard shut his binder of research first and nodded. "I for one am convinced." The way he smiled at the two of them made Aella think that Barker's suspicions were correct and that the vampire had already guessed that the two of them were mates. This was just his way of showing that he supported them.

"The evidence is overwhelming," Shelly said. "Though I do still have some reservations."

Barker cleared his throat. "Is there anything we can do to help that?"

Aella wanted to add that they'd do anything they needed to. She knew how important it was to Barker that he kept his seat, and she wanted hers just as much.

"I think we need to instigate some rules if we allow you to both keep your seats," she said.

"What? You can't seriously be considering letting the two of them keep their seats?" Something between shock and anger lingered in Drummond's voice. "They've been lying to us since Aella joined the Council."

"Is your dislike for Aella really so strong that you'll let two excellent Council members leave over it?" Shelly's exasperation was almost as strong as the dragon's hatred.

Aella's stomach sank. She'd always suspected that the dragon shifter had something against her, but having it confirmed by one of the other Council members was even worse than she'd imagined it would be.

"I have nothing against the girl," Drummond countered.

"Then I'd appreciate it if you stopped referring to me as a girl," Aella said. "I may be younger than you are, but I've spent my life preparing for a seat on the High Council. I've wanted this for as long as I've known how the Councils worked. Which is something I suspect you know or you wouldn't have approved me to take the empty seat in the first place."

Barker beamed with pride at her, but didn't say anything. She was grateful for that, she didn't want it to seem as if she wasn't able to fight her own battles when she needed to.

"I'll have you know that I was outvoted," Drummond responded tartly."

"And you're about to be again," Shelly muttered, clearly annoyed with the dragon shifter's attitude. "I vote that the two of you can retain your Council seats, and that each new mated partnership between Council members should be evaluated on a case by case situation."

"I second that," Richard said with a smile on his face.

Aella breathed a sigh of relief.

"Thank you," Barker said. "We'll obviously work with you to establish some rules to counteract the bias."

"That's acceptable," Richard said. "I'm sure it will take us a while to get into the swing of things, but once we are, the Council will be stronger for it."

Drummond scowled at them all, but didn't say a word. Aella wondered how long the dragon shifter would stay on the High Council after this. Perhaps forever. He'd been there a long time already. This couldn't be the first time he'd disagreed so firmly with the other Council members.

"I have a meeting," he announced, getting to his feet and making his way to the door without another word.

"I actually do too," Shelly said, clearing up her papers and getting ready to follow. "Congratulations on your mating," she said to them.

"Thank you," Aella responded. "And for your support just now."

The other woman's lips curved into a smile. "I didn't do it for you. I didn't even do it to get the better of Drummond. I did it because it's best for the High Council. That is always my number one priority."

"Mine too," Aella assured her.

"Then I don't think this will be a problem at all." She didn't wait for a response and left the room.

"You found what you were looking for, then?" Richard said, a satisfied smile on his face.

"You knew it was there, didn't you?" Barker asked.

"I suspected. But it was never the right time for me to bring the issue up. But the archaic rules need to change, and this was the perfect chance to make that a reality."

"Thank you for your help," Barker said. "If you hadn't pointed us in the right direction…"

"Then you'd have found another way," he pointed out. "Anyway, I must be going, I'm meeting Tabby for lunch." He disappeared without another door, leaving the two of them alone in the Council rooms.

Aella turned to Barker with a wide smile on her face. "We did it."

"We did." He stepped close and pulled her into his arms. "Which I think means that it's time to celebrate."

"I like the sound of that. What did you have in mind?"

A glint of wickedness entered his eyes.

"Here?" she asked, not wanting to admit how much she liked the idea. "We shouldn't…"

"And yet it would be so fun." His gaze dropped to her lips, and she knew that she was going to give in to his suggestion.

She wrapped her arms around him and pulled him close to her. His lips crushed against hers and she started to lose herself in him, no longer caring where they were. All that mattered was that she was his and he was hers.

And nothing would be able to keep them apart.

EPILOGUE

BARKER

BARKER PARKED the car by the entrance to the race track, marvelling at how much this place had changed in such a small amount of time. Not that long ago it had been nothing but a field, and now it was something so much more. In a few months, it would be teeming with paranormals as they launched the world's first paranormal only motor racing track.

It was truly something the High Council could be proud of.

"It's perfect weather today," Aella said as she got out of the car.

Barker glanced at the dark grey clouds in the sky and let out a bemused chuckle. Of course she'd think this was perfect, she was a nymph born beneath a storm.

"Let's hope it's a little bit sunnier for when we open to the public," Barker said.

Aella smiled knowingly. "I suppose. Though a little bit of water will be good for the drama of the racing."

"You've changed your tune from not understanding why this is even a thing," he teased.

"I like Jax," she admitted. "She explained a lot of why she chose to race with me, and it helped me start to understand it."

"I see." It didn't surprise him that Aella's opinion had changed. She was an open-minded person, it was one of the things that made her a good Council member. But he still liked seeing it in action.

"Ah, there she is now," Aella said, waving at a woman a few feet away.

Barker raised an eyebrow. He wasn't sure what he'd expected of a tortoise shifting race driver, but the woman heading towards him wasn't it. He'd never have been able to guess her profession if he hadn't already known.

Aella hurried over, with Barker following quickly behind.

"Hi, I'm Aella, this is Barker, we're representatives of the High Council," Aella said with just the right amount of friendliness and professionalism.

"I'm Jax." The woman held out her hand and shook hands with Aella first and then Barker. "I think we've spoken on the phone."

"We have," Aella responded. "I'm glad you could make it down here, we need to go through what you need for the opening event."

"I can take you through it now if you want?"

"That sounds good." Aella turned to Barker. "Will you be all right doing what you need to without us?"

"Of course. You remember what the Council said."

She beamed at him, an expression that lit up her face and made him fall for her that little bit more.

He watched as the two women walked away, unable to take his eyes off the storm nymph who had stolen his heart. He'd known she was his mate the moment the two of them had met in the High Council chambers, but he'd fallen in love with her over the course of the year since. Seeing the intelligence and fairness with which she judged and treated others had made him realise just why they'd been matched together.

His world was better for having Aella Dentro in it, and he had no doubt that was true for the entire paranormal community too. She was a force to be reckoned with, and he never wanted to be without her.

Thank you for reading *Resisting Her Shifter*, I hope you enjoyed it. If you want to read more about the events at the race track, you can in *The Tortoise's Race*: http://books2read.com/thetortoisesrace

Or you can return to the beginning of The Paranormal Council series and read about Aella's sister in *The Dryad's Pawprint*: http://books2read.com/thedryadspawprint

AUTHOR NOTE

Thank you for reading *Resisting Her Shifter*, I hope you enjoyed it.

Aella has been a character I've known a lot about since I first started writing books in *The Paranormal Council Universe*. She's the sister of the main character in book one, *The Dryad's Pawprint*, and made it clear from the get-go that the High Council was her goal as a career. I've known for years that her fated mate was a snow leopard, but I didn't know anything else about him until I was writing some of the later books set in the universe.

If you want to learn more about some of the other characters or organisations mentioned in *Resisting Her Shifter*, then here's where you can find them:

- Richard meets his mate, Tabitha, during the events of *Blood and Deceit*.

- Narcissa (Cissy) and Darius and the exploits of *The Necromancer Council* are detailed in the series of the same name.

- Arabella (Ari) and Bjorn are the main characters in *The Vixen's Bark*.

- The setting up and work of the *Paranormal Criminal Investigations* department is explored in the series of the same name.

I'm so glad I got the opportunity to finally write Aella's story, and I hope you enjoyed it!

If you want to keep up to date with new releases and other news, you can join my Facebook Reader Group or mailing list.

Stay safe & happy reading!

- Laura

ALSO BY LAURA GREENWOOD

Signed Paperback & Merchandise:

You can find signed paperbacks, hardcovers, and merchandise based on my series (including stickers, magnets, face masks, and more!) via my website: https://www.authorlauragreenwood.co.uk/p/shop.html

Series List:

* denotes a completed series

The Obscure World

A paranormal & urban fantasy world where supernaturals live out in the open alongside humans. Each series can be read on its own, but there are cameos from past characters and mentions of previous events.

Ashryn Barker* - Grimalkin Academy: Kittens* - Grimalkin Academy: Catacombs* - City Of Blood* - Grimalkin Vampires* - Supernatural Retrieval Agency* - The Black Fan - Sabre Woods Academy* - Scythe Grove Academy* - The Shifter Season - Cauldron Coffee Shop - Broomstick Bakery - Obscure Academy - Stonerest Academy - Obscure World: Holidays - Harker Academy

The Forgotten Gods World

A fantasy romance world based on Egyptian mythology.
Each series can be read on its own, but there are cameos
from past characters and mentions of previous events.

The Queen of Gods* - Forgotten Gods - Forgotten
Gods: Origins*

The Egyptian Empire

A modern fantasy world set in an alternative timeline
where the Egyptian Empire never fell.

The Apprentice Of Anubis

* * *

The Grimm World

A fantasy fairy tale romance world. Each series can be

read on its own, but there are cameos from past characters and mentions of previous events.

Grimm Academy* - Fate Of The Crown* - Once Upon An Academy* - The Princess Competition

* * *

The Paranormal Council World

A paranormal romance & urban fantasy world where paranormals are hidden away from the human world, and are in search of their fated mates. Each series can be read on its own, but there are cameos from past characters and mentions of previous events.

The Paranormal Council Series* - The Fae Queens* - Paranormal Criminal Investigations* - MatchMater Paranormal Dating App* - The Necromancer Council* - Return Of The Fae*

* * *

Other Series

Beyond The Curse* - Untold Tales* - The Dragon

Duels* - Rosewood Academy - ME* - Speed Dating
With The Denizens Of The Underworld (shared world)
- Seven Wardens* (co-written with Skye MacKinnon) -
Tales Of Clan Robbins (co-written with L.A. Boruff) -

Firehouse Witches* (co-written with Lacey Carter
Andersen & L.A. Boruff) - Purple Oasis (co-written
series with Arizona Tape) - Valentine Pride* (co-written
with L.A. Boruff) - Magic and Metaphysics Academy*
(co-written with L.A. Boruff)

Twin Souls Universe

A paranormal romance & urban fantasy world co-written
with Arizona Tape. Each series can be read on its own,
but there are cameos from past characters and mentions
of previous events.

Twin Souls* - Dragon Soul* - The Renegade Dragons* -
The Vampire Detective* - Amethyst's Wand Shop
Mysteries - The Necromancer Morgue Mysteries

ABOUT LAURA GREENWOOD

Laura is a USA Today Bestselling Author of paranormal, fantasy, urban fantasy, and contemporary romance. When she's not writing, she drinks a lot of tea, tries to resist French macarons, and works towards a diploma in Egyptology. She lives in the UK, where most of her books are set. Laura specialises in quick reads, whether you're looking for a swoonworthy romance for the bath, or an action-packed adventure for your latest journey, you'll find the perfect match amongst her books!

Follow the Author

- Website: www.authorlauragreenwood.co.uk
- Mailing List: www.authorlauragreenwood.co.uk/p/mailing-list-sign-up.html
- Facebook Group: http://facebook.com/groups/theparanormalcouncil

- Facebook Page: http://facebook.com/authorlauragreenwood
- Bookbub: www.bookbub.com/authors/laura-greenwood

Printed in Great Britain
by Amazon